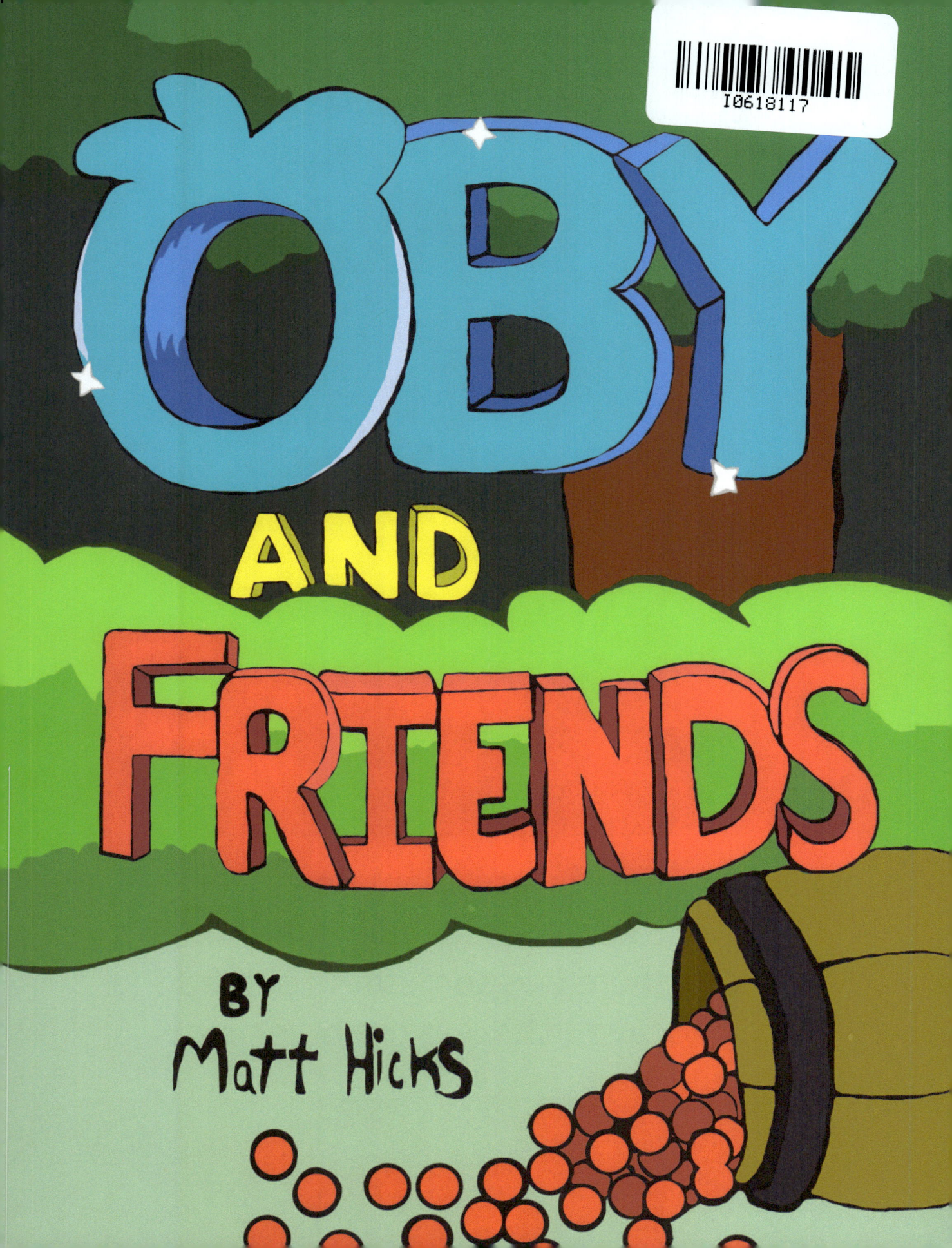

OBY AND FRIENDS

BY Matt Hicks

There was a giant berry tree in the center of the island. But on this day, there was something behind the leaves, shaking the branches.

"It's another berry!" Oby chirped excitedly,
"It's a red one too."

THUD!
Oby landed in a heap with arms
and legs in all directions!
"OUCH! That wasn't fun at all!"

Opal followed Oby, as he walked
over to one of his berry barrels.
He laid back and gave out a growling yawn
before taking his nap.

Oby thought. . .

And he thought. . .

SNAP

Until. . .

Back at his castle,
Oby worked away on his idea,
determined to get more of those
delicious berries from the trees.

"This Claw-Grabber-Catcher will do the job."

SNAP

"With this rig, I can simply VACUUM the berries into my backpack."

But Oby found the vacuum would suck anything into his backpack!

By nightfall, Oby
was discouraged. His ideas
weren't working and he
felt like he had been
defeated.
He decided to sit on
his anvil and think.

"When you are **whopping ready for a change, you always find a way.** And I know **when you get charged up, there's no stopping you.**"

"I don't want to go back to falling
out of trees." said Oby.
"Yes, I'm ready for a change!"

Oby hammered and welded, and
he hammered some more. He worked happily
through the night, humming his favorite songs
What a night it was!

Oby was as happy as he could be. His work had proven as good as his imagination.
He gave the robot a big hug.
The robot didn't understand, for he had never before HAD a hug,
yet somehow, he knew it was a good thing.

"Are you kidding me? I can pick them quicker than you can say my name, 'Scrapzoid Scrapernicus'. But instead of struggling with that, you can call me 'SCRAPS' "

Scraps was eager to see the berry trees.
So they left the castle in a rush.

"Here we are, Scraps." Oby whistled,
"Many of the berries are hard for me
to reach and. . ."
But Scraps was already picking,
and picking FAST! He could stretch his arms high,
bend the branches, and pick all
the berries they needed.

And while they picked, they sang a few happy tunes.

"You are amazing too, Oby." Scraps said.
"Everybody has a talent. Mine is helping
friends and, well, who knows what else.
And Opal gives inspiration, wisdom and
kindness.
I think we make a fine team!"

www.ingramcontent.com/pod-product-compliance
Lightning Source LLC
Chambersburg PA
CBHW040959170626
46815CB00002B/74